This book belongs to:

This 1989 Muppet Press book is published by Longmeadow Press.
Distributed by Checkerboard Press,
a division of Macmillan, Inc.

Printed in United States
ISBN 002-689263-4
a b c d e f g h

The Fraggles Cooperate

by Harry Ross   illustrated by Larry Di Fiori

Muppet Press

Cog is working all alone.

Ratchet helps her lift the stone.

Friends lend friends a helping hand.
Cooperation's really grand!

Boober's busy brewing stew.
That's hard work for one to do.

Wembley goes to get a spoon—
They'll be eating dinner soon.

One small Doozer builds
a spire.

Two small Doozers make it higher.

Doozer duos get things done.
Two are twice as fast as one.

What a mess—dirt everywhere!
All the Fraggles do their share.
In a minute, things are neat.
Cooperation can't be beat.

This pogo stick goes fast and high.
Fraggles wait to have a try.

Cooperation, as we learn, means:
Do not push—please take your turn.

When Mom is mopping up the floor,
She needs your help to do the chore.

Cooperation feels so nice—
She doesn't have to ask you twice.

And when you go to bed at night,
And close your tired eyes so tight,
You'll dream about your busy day—
A little work, a little play.

You'll know, when every day is done,
That helping people makes life fun.

And so, in case you haven't heard—
COOPERATION is the word!